Loon at Northwood Lake

SMITHSONIAN'S BACKYARD

For Lelli — E.R.

For my wife, Elizabeth — T.O.

Book copyright © 1997 Trudy Corporation, 353 Main Avenue, Norwalk, CT 06851,
and the Smithsonian Institution, Washington, DC 20560.

Soundprints is a division of Trudy Corporation, Norwalk, Connecticut.

Book Design: Shields & Partners, Westport, CT

First Edition 1997
10 9 8 7 6 5 4 3 2 1
Printed in Singapore

Acknowledgements:
   Our very special thanks to Dr. Gary Graves of the Division of Birds at the
Smithsonian Institution's National Museum of Natural History for his curatorial review.

Library of Congress Cataloging-in-Publication Data

Ring, Elizabeth, 1920-

Loon at Northwood Lake / by Elizabeth Ring; illustrated by Taylor Oughton.
        p.   cm.
Summary: Loon and his mate protect their chicks from curious people, egg-hunting eagles
and hawks, and ferocious pike throughout a summer at Northwood Lake.
        ISBN 1-56899-393-5
1. Loons — Juvenile fiction. [1. Loons — Fiction.]
I. Oughton, Taylor, 1925-   ill. II. Title.
        PZ10.3.R48Lo 1997   96-39101
        [Fic]—dc21   CIP
                                                   AC

Loon at Northwood Lake

by Elizabeth Ring
Illustrated by Taylor Oughton

Soundprints™

Where Children Discover...

4

A gray April sky hangs over Northwood Lake and the log cottage near the lake's ice-crusted shore. Loon circles high. Below, all is quiet, and the big bird glides down. He lands on the cold water and skids to a foamy stop.

He hoots twice, as if claiming this small north-country lake as his own.

Loon has flown far from his winter home on the Atlantic Ocean. Hungry, he dives, spies a small perch, and snatches the fish crosswise in his long, pointed beak. He gulps it down whole, underwater.

Rising to the surface, he stretches, waggling each webbed foot out behind him. Then he naps, floating.

Though dozing, he hears the moose and raccoon rustling among the spruce trees onshore, and the tree frogs peeping. Loon is always on guard.

Late the next day, Loon welcomes his mate. She too has flown far from her own winter home. She looks like Loon's twin sister with her black-and-white back, her ruby-red eyes, and, around her neck, a necklace of white patches and a collar of white stripes.

The loons greet each other, rubbing heads, dipping and tossing their beaks. They're together again, at their old summer home.

Like two figure skaters, the pair swims side by side along the shore, seeking this year's nesting place.

They come to a small, quiet island, far from the homes of hungry skunks and raccoons.

The birds stumble onto the shore like big-footed clowns. Their feet are for swimming, not walking.

They fling a nest together with beakfuls of grass, twigs, and water plants. It looks like a big, sloppy salad.

In a few days, Loon's mate lays two olive-brown eggs. For four weeks, Loon and his mate take turns sitting on the nest. They keep the eggs warm and shoo off egg-hunting eagles and hawks.

Then, on a cool, breezy day in May, one loon chick hatches, the next day another.

"*Hut-hut*," clucks Loon, coaxing each loonling into the lake. Born swimmers, the waterproofed chicks bob on the water like fuzzy ping-pong balls. Their parents lead them to an island cove to feed.

"*Cheep, cheep*," the chicks beg.

Loon and his mate poke insects and bits of fish and crayfish toward their small beaks.

Stuffed, the chicks paddle contentedly on the shadowy water, unaware that a huge hungry fish lurks below. But both Loon and his mate spy the ferocious pike.

Loon's mate screeches a warning. Loon dives, his dagger-beak aimed at the pike. His powerful legs and big feet churn as he zooms underwater, driving the pike far away.

When Loon pops up for air, he hears his mate's call.
"*Aaaah-oooooh-aaaahhh!*" she wails.
He races to her side. A loonling is missing!
The parents dart here and there, keeping the safe chick
in sight. They circle and dive. The lost chick is not on the
water, not on shore, not caught in the weeds below.

Then, from downshore, comes a faint *"Cheep, Cheep-Cheep!"* Loon stays by the safe chick as his mate dashes toward the wee sound. It's the lost loonling, peeking out from the reeds.

All four together again, Loon's mate lowers herself in the water. The cold, tired chicks scramble onto her back for a warm, safe, feathery ferry-boat ride.

One puffy-cloud June afternoon, shouts and laughter ring out from the summer cottage on Northwood Lake's shore. Loon has heard those cottage sounds before.

But today something is new — something that looks like a gigantic fish. It glides out from the dock and moves steadily toward the loons' feeding place.

Too close! Too close!

Loon screams a shrill warning. Flapping his wings, he stands straight up on the water and slaps his feet furiously.

The canoe turns and slips away. Loon hears low, gentle voices. After that, the canoe never again comes too near.

As steamy August crawls by, Loon watches his chicks struggle to fly. *Splash! Flap!* Their wings grow stronger each day.

One day, *Pat-pat-swoosh!* Up go the young birds, on their own at last. Loon's guardian work is done.

Each loon now wanders the lake alone. Many nights, though, when light spills from the cottage windows, they call to each other.

"*Ahaa-ooo-ooo-ahh*," Loon wails.

Loon's mate calls back.

The young loons chime in: "*Hoo-hah! Aaah-hoo-oooahh!*"

Sometimes, loons from other lakes join the chorus until the hills echo with wails, yodels, and loony laughter.

Soft "*oooohs*" and "*aahhhhs*" come from the cottage porch, too.

The concerts go on, into the fall.

Late in frosty, gold-leafed October, Loon starts changing his black-and-white feathers for his gray winter coat. He's restless. It's time to head back to his winter home on the Atlantic Ocean.

Early one cold, windy morning, he skitters, *pat-pat-pat-pat*, on the water, splashing his feet and beating his wings. He finally gets up enough speed and lifts off, wings flapping hard, into the gray, cloudy sky.

Loon circles the lake twice, climbing higher and higher. He takes one last look down at his summer home. Below, his mate and young ones feed, by themselves. They'll soon leave the lake, too, when each is ready.

Before long, ice will coat Northwood Lake. A stillness will fall on the lake and log cottage — until the spring sun brings back the loons and the laughter next year.

About the Loon

The common loon is known for its bold black-and-white spots and stripes, and for its dark red eyes. Each loon's necklace and collar are unique, as individual as a person's fingerprints. The red color of their eyes may help loons see better underwater. Sight is their keenest sense, and they find fish to eat by swimming with their eyes just below the surface of the water.

A pair of loons usually raises one or two loonlings each year. At the end of the summer the loonlings are old enough to take care of themselves. The parents' feathers change from black-and-white to brown, and all of the loons fly to separate winter homes along the shores of the Atlantic or Pacific Oceans or the Gulf of Mexico. In the spring, the loon parents will likely return to the same lake to raise another pair of loonlings. But the children, now full grown, will find their own lakes and mates.

Except when they are nesting, loons live their entire lives on water. But being well adapted for water can be a problem on land. Loons' feet are placed so far back on their bodies that they have a hard time walking. They often scoot on their bellies, pushing with their feet, or use their wings as "crutches." Loons' heavy bones make it hard for them to take off and fly. They run on the surface of the water for up to a quarter of a mile, flapping their wings until they have enough speed to take off.

Loons' strange behavior and their eerie nighttime calls have intrigued people and inspired legends for hundreds of years. To some, the wails, yodels, and "loony laughter" sound insane; to others, like howling wolves. Once, the Cree Indians believed the ghostly calls were from dead warriors barred from heaven.

Glossary

cove: a small, watery, cup-shaped place along a shoreline, often sheltered by reeds.

crayfish: a small, hard-shelled crustacean that looks like a little lobster.

loonling: a baby loon, up to about 10 weeks old.

perch: a long, slender fish; many are yellow with dark bars on their sides.

yodel: a warbling sound that goes quickly back and forth between high and low notes.

Points of Interest in this Book

pp. 6-7 loons sleep at intervals throughout the day, usually with their beaks tucked under a wing.

pp. 12-13 bald eagle.

pp. 14-15 blue flags in bloom.

pp. 14-15, 18-23 loonlings with downy gray feathers.

pp. 20-21 bullhead pond lilies.

pp. 24-25 loonlings with adolescent feathers.

pp. 28-29 Loon with winter colors.